"One day I heard one of my son's friends say: 'If Mum didn't ask so many questions, I wouldn't have to tell her so many lies!' I think *Cry Wolf* developed from that really. . ."

Susan Gates

Also by Susan Gates in Scholastic Press:

Criss Cross

.

Chapter One

Before Danny went into his house, he searched his own pockets.

Lately his mum had been really suspicious. If there was 50p in his pocket that he wasn't supposed to have, she would say: "Where did this come from, Danny? You didn't steal it, did you?"

If she found a dead match she would say: "You haven't started smoking again, have you? I knew I couldn't trust you."

Danny pulled out the linings of his pockets and brushed off the dust. Mum might think it was cigarette ash.

You had to be on the alert with Mum. It was like constant guerrilla warfare. If he had a hiding place, she would find it. She searched his school bag. She even felt inside the pillowcase on his bed. She was keener than a sniffer dog.

She said: "I don't want to be like this, Danny. I hate checking up on you. I want to be able to trust you. But I obviously can't, can I?"

And Danny protested: "But I'm not doing anything wrong, Mum. I'm not smoking any more. I won't play truant again. I'm being good!"

But she didn't believe him.

Danny pushed open his front door. He barely had time to unsling his school bag from his shoulders before Mum pounced.

"Oh no," thought Danny. "What now?"

It was true that two weeks ago he'd skipped school for the day. He'd invited his friend Nico round. They'd pinched some bottles of Dad's home-brew and watched some videos. And made a mess of the kitchen making pancakes. And Mum had come home early from work and caught them.

But that didn't make him a *criminal*, did it?

Yet all the trouble had started from that day.

Mum had reacted really badly. She had gone way over the top.

She thought Danny was "out of control". She thought he'd been getting up to all sorts of bad things behind her back.

Danny had protested, "Honest, Mum, I won't play truant again. I just did it once to see what it was like. And it was really boring, OK?"

But his mum didn't believe him. And, worse than this, she decided it was partly her fault. She decided that she hadn't kept a close enough eye on Danny.

She was certainly making up for it now.

Danny sighed as Mum strode down the hall to meet him. Her eyes had a dangerous glint in them. His mum was only little. He was much taller than her now. But, when she got mad, she was like a hurricane on the loose.

"And what is this, may I ask?" she said, waving something in his face. It was a black baseball cap.

Danny gulped. He couldn't help looking guilty. Even though, this time, he had nothing to be guilty about.

"Well," said his mum, tapping her tiny size 3 trainers, "I'm waiting for an explanation. It's not your cap is it, Danny? Where did you get it from?"

"I didn't nick it from a shop, if that's what you think."

Danny cursed the day that he and Nico had played truant. Back in the golden days, when Mum had been laid-back and easy-going, she would never have noticed the cap. Now everything he did made her twitch.

"I'm still waiting," said Mum.

Danny opened his mouth like a goldfish. No words came out. So he closed it again. For one crazy moment he was tempted to say that he had stolen it. He knew his mum would believe that because these days she only believed bad things about him.

"I found it," said Danny, shrugging hopelessly.

"Don't lie to me, Danny. Even I can tell it's not an ordinary cap. It looks like a very expensive one."

"I did, honest. It was just lying in the gutter, you know, by the Chinese take-away, the *Rain Flower*. So I just rescued it and brushed the dirt off and put it on my head."

Mum was right – it wasn't an ordinary cap. Danny knew that as soon as he'd picked it up. He'd never seen one like it in any of the sports shops. It looked like shiny black leather. But it was made of soft material that felt good on your head. And it had a big silver star on the front like a Sheriff's star. Even the silver star wasn't ordinary. It was some sort of hologram. When the light caught it, it shimmered with rainbow colours, like an oil slick on a wet road.

"You don't expect me to believe that do you?" said Mum. "That you just found it? Why didn't you take it to the police? It might belong to some poor old-aged pensioner."

"Old-aged pensioners don't wear caps like this!"

"I'll take it to the police then. Where did you say you found it? Outside the *Rain Flower*? And what day was it?"

"Err, Wednesday night."

"You were grounded on Wednesday. How could you have found it on Wednesday night? You didn't go out."

His mum's nose twitched, like a bloodhound's on the trail of a stink.

"Well, it was some other day then!" bawled Danny, wild with exasperation. "I don't know, do I? I can't remember, can I? I just found it, that's all!"

"I'll take it to the police station."

Danny was almost a hundred per cent certain she was bluffing. But you could never be quite sure. His mum was the most honest person he knew. So honest that, if she found a lump of chewing gum stuck to the bottom of her shoe, she'd probably try and find out who it belonged to.

"Well, I'll just keep this cap for the moment," said Mum, tucking it under her arm. "Until we sort all this out."

Danny groaned. "Look, I've told you and told you, there's nothing to sort out. I found it, that's all. I don't nick stuff from shops. Except when I was a kid I nicked some chocolate bars, OK? But I don't do that no more. I've grown out of it. I don't even smoke no more. I'm being so good I can't hardly believe it myself! I'm being so good I'm really boring! But just because I played truant for one day, you think I'm a serial killer or something! What's the point of being good, eh? I might as well not bother!"

Mum's face was still grey with worry. Her lips were tight.

She said, in a small grim voice, "But I blame myself, Danny. It's my fault. I should have seen all this coming."

"It's not your fault, it's *my* fault!" roared Danny, almost exploding with frustration. "It's nothing to do with you. It's *my* responsibility. It's *my* fault I played truant!"

But Mum had already stalked off into the kitchen.

Danny groaned again, a deep gut-wrenching groan. "I just wish she'd leave me alone, like she did before," he thought.

But there was no hope of that. Mum was on his case. She was watching his every move. And every private corner of his life was lit up, as if by searchlights.

Chapter Two

Danny had forgotten to spray on his *Adidas* deodorant. So he lifted up his arms and gave his armpits a couple of quick squirts through his school shirt. He had a frantic burst of play on his computer game, *pow, pow, pow*. Then he hoisted his school bag on to his shoulder. And slouched, very very slowly, slower than a three-toed tree sloth, down the stairs—

"Danny? You'll be late for school."

It was not his mum's usual shriek.

"Red alert! Red alert!" warned Danny's brain.

And when he oozed into the kitchen for breakfast, one look at his mum's face confirmed it.

She was in an understanding mood.

"Oh Christ," thought Danny, flopping into a chair.

Mum gave him her sweetest smile.

Danny gulped.

"Have some cornflakes," said Mum.

She dumped some into his bowl, sloshed in the milk.

Then sat down, facing him, her chin in her hands.

She was staring at him – without blinking.

"*Crunch, crunch*," went Danny, with his head down.

"You know," began Mum, "if you've got anything to tell me, Danny, anything at all, I'm ready to listen."

"*Nurrgh*," grunted Danny through his cornflakes.

"Sure?" said Mum, in a voice like honey. "Any problems you want to share? About where that cap came from? About anything else?" she cooed. "I won't be angry, honestly. I won't be shocked. You can tell me anything."

"Nope," Danny mumbled.

Mum looked disappointed. She sounded irritated. "What, nothing at all?"

"Nope," said Danny. Then he added, "Look, there's no need to worry about me. Everything's under control. OK?"

He hated being hassled at breakfast time. He hated having heart-to-hearts this early in the morning. He didn't wake up until break time at least. Some days he didn't wake up until bedtime.

"Look," said Mum. "I'm making time for you, Danny." She checked her watch. "I should be getting ready for work. But I'm sitting here with nothing to do but listen. I just want to help." Her eyes slid to her watch again.

"Oh no," thought Danny, looking round for some way to escape. But Mum had him cornered.

"So isn't there anything you want to tell me?"

"Like what?" asked Danny, dopily. He could have bitten his tongue off as soon as he'd said it. But he was about as sharp as silly string in the mornings.

Mum shrugged. "Oh, you know," she said, casually. "Like drugs, or, you know problems with sex – things you don't understand."

"Nope, nope, nope," said Danny, frantically. "Except, look at my muscles!" He rolled up his sleeve and made his biceps pop. "See that? Nico's got some weights and I been lifting them at his house. I'll be getting a six-pack soon. Go on, punch my stomach. Go on, hard as you like!"

But his mum wasn't going to be side-tracked.

"There must be *something* you're not telling me,"

she insisted. "We must have something more important to discuss than the state of your muscles. And, anyway, what were you doing at Nico's house? I told you to keep away from him."

"For Heaven's sake!" bawled Danny. He leapt up. His chair crashed behind him. He made wild sweeping movements with his arms as if he was fighting off a swarm of angry wasps.

"I wish you'd leave me alone! I'm not even awake yet! I was just sitting here all peaceful, just relaxing, eating my cornflakes, minding my own business. . . All right, I do drugs, loads and loads of 'em. All right, I'm in a gang and we go mugging old ladies for their caps, right? We do it for laughs. Ha! Ha! OK? All right, I think babies come from Mothercare! That what you want to hear?"

For a nanosecond Mum looked shocked. Then her eyes narrowed. "You're joking, aren't you?" she said. "Aren't you?"

Danny spat out a disgusted: "For God's sake!"

He gave his mum his killer shark stare from under scowling black eyebrows.

His mum stared back. But the expression on her face was bewildered, like a little lost child. Danny recognized that expression. It was on his own face a lot of the time.

His anger drained away like water down a plug hole.

He hated being investigated. But he also hated to see Mum unhappy. So he gave her a hug.

"Poor little Mum," he said, scrubbing her short spiky hair. She used to do that to him before he got too tall. "Don't worry, little Mum. I'm not in any trouble, honest. I'm thirteen now. I can look after myself. Look, I'm bigger than you, I can even lift you up!"

And he grabbed his mum round the waist and heaved her a few centimetres off the floor.

Mum struggled and laughed.

Danny grinned. It was great to hear his mum laughing again.

He plonked her back on her feet.

"Bye."

"Bye, Danny."

"Catch you later."

"Bye."

Danny yanked open the freezer door, grabbed a blue ice-pop, then clumped across the kitchen.

Suddenly, he turned round. He did have something

to ask Mum. He'd been plucking up courage to ask her for two days now.

"You haven't told Dad, have you?" he asked her. "When he phoned up from Spain you didn't tell him, did you? About me playing truant and stuff? I won't do it again, Mum. I didn't miss anything important – it was only maths and cross-country running."

"No, I didn't tell him. And I'm not going to tell him either. I said everything here was fine. Your dad's got enough to worry about."

"Thanks, Mum," said Danny, gratefully.

Danny's mum waited for the door to slam. For a few minutes she stood in the middle of the kitchen. She wanted to trust Danny. She really did. And she knew she might find something that would ruin her day. But all the same, she came to a sudden decision. And galloped up the stairs to search his bedroom.

Chapter Three

Outside, Danny's friend Nico was waiting for him. They grunted at each other.

"Hi."

"Aw wight?" replied Nico.

They trudged silently along the pavement. Danny ripped his ice-pop open with his teeth.

Nico didn't come to the door any more. Danny's mum had decided she didn't approve of him.

"That Ben Nicholson," she told Danny, "it was his idea to play truant, wasn't it? Sometimes you're very easily led, Danny."

"I'm not easily led!" bawled Danny. "It was *my* idea. Right? *My* responsibility. I keep telling you and telling you!"

But Mum just said, "I always thought Nico was a bad influence."

It was true Nico wasn't every mummy's dream. He looked like a shambling bear. He had hair like red fuzz and hands like shovels. And he didn't have much conversation.

"Aw wight?" he said again to Danny.

Danny winced as slushy blue ice touched one of his sensitive teeth.

"No, you mong," he said.

"Whatsamatter then?"

"It's my mum," groaned Danny. "She wants to understand me! And she's taken my cap, you know, that really neat one I found! And she's watching every move I make. She's like Sherlock Holmes. She's probably searching my bedroom right now. She won't find nothing though," said Danny with a grin. "I've made sure about that."

Nicky shook his big shaggy head in sympathy.

"Have your parents," Danny asked Nico, "ever tried to understand you?"

Nico just shrugged. "What for?" he said.

"That's exactly it!" cried Danny, flinging his arms wide, as if he was on a stage, making a big, dramatic speech. "It's so *pointless*, isn't it? I mean, the more Mum finds out the more she worries. So why does she want to find things out? Why doesn't she just stop trying to find out, then she'd have nothing to worry about, would she? And everyone would be happy again. I mean, it's obvious, isn't it. Just think about it!"

Nico thought about it, then frowned and gave up. He said, "Take a look at this," and screwed his neck round so Danny could see the back of his head.

"That's very artistic," said Danny.

Nico had a Christmas tree shaved into the back of his head.

"It's not Christmas, though," said Danny. "It's not Christmas for six months."

Nico shrugged. "So I'm early."

"Who did it?" asked Danny.

"My mum," said Nico. "Good, isn't it?"

Danny's brain tried to grapple with this. He tried to imagine *his* mum shaving a Christmas tree into the back of his head. But his mind was like a black hole. He just couldn't imagine it. It was about as probable as snow in August.

Danny had tried explaining to Mum about Nico. He tried to tell her that going round with Nico was the best insurance policy you could have. Danny was small and skinny. He hated fighting. When bullies saw him their eyes lit up. But with Nico beside him no one dared touch him. Nico was his personal bodyguard.

And, besides, Danny liked him. His mum couldn't understand that.

"Isn't he in bottom band?" she said once.

"So?" said Danny.

"Well," said Mum, looking embarrassed, "er, don't you want to go around with someone you can *talk* to?"

"Nico isn't thick, if that's what you mean."

"I didn't say that."

But Danny knew that's what she meant.

"Hey Nico!" said Danny, giving him a swipe with his school bag.

Nico dodged it easily, went into a boxer's crouch and pummelled at Danny with his head down.

"Geroff, geroff!" laughed Danny.

It was only a joke fight. Nico could do a lot of damage with those great fists. But he wouldn't dream of hurting Danny. The blows he landed were deliberately gentle.

After a quick scuffle they walked on.

Danny said, "But it's getting on my nerves, Nico. All this hassle Mum's giving me. I can't get away with nothing. I've got to stop her worrying about me. I hate it when she worries. Since Dad went to work in Spain she's been even worse. Like she's got to worry twice as hard or something. Like she's got the whole world on her shoulders!"

Danny felt a nasty twinge of guilt when he spoke about his dad. When Dad left three weeks ago to work on a building site in Spain, his last words to Danny had been, "Look after your mum. Don't give her any worry."

And Danny had said, "I won't, Dad. That's a promise."

But he'd already broken that promise.

"Well," Nico was saying, "it's obvious what to do. You got to make her think you're being a good boy."

Danny puffed out his cheeks in a sigh. "Fat chance," he said. "She thinks I'm Jack the Ripper or something."

"Like for instance," Nico continued, grinning, "you shouldn't be hanging around with naughty boys like me, should you? You should be hanging round with good boys. I bet that's what she's told you, isn't it?"

Danny looked embarrassed. But there wasn't any bitterness in Nico's voice. He knew Danny's mum didn't approve of him. He didn't resent it. He seemed almost to expect it.

"Hang on! I've just got an idea," said Danny, sounding surprised. "What you just said, it's given me this really class idea. You're brilliant, Nico. You're a mastermind, you mong!"

They walked a few steps.

"What does 'mong' mean?" asked Nico.

"Oh, you know," said Danny, "it means crazy person or something. Everyone's calling their mates a mong."

"I thought they were calling each other spaff-heads. I thought spaff-head meant crazy."

"No," said Danny, shaking his head, "you're so old-fashioned, Nico. Spaff-head was last week's word."

Chapter Four

Danny's eleven-year-old brother was writing stories. His real name was Jonathan. But nobody called him that. His nickname was Tiddler. But nobody called him that either. Everyone called him Tid.

Tid was sitting in the bedroom he shared with Danny, typing his story on to the computer. He had a pile of Smarties next to him. He ate one Smartie then typed a few words, ate another, then typed some more. By the time he had eaten all the blue Smarties he'd written this:

I'm going to start this story with once upon a time. I know that's not original or anything but that's how it starts, OK? So once upon a time there was this creature. He roamed the countryside. He was called Wolf but actually he was half-man and half-wolf and he's a monster and you'd better be scared of him if you know what's good for you.

He is your worst nightmare.

This is how you recognize Wolf. He prowls around in the dark, specially in graveyards. He's got silver teeth that are made of metal and yellow eyes and he is slightly not to say totally crazy. And his victims are INNOCENT children!

Anyway once upon a time Wolf and all his wolf mates were out looking for HUMAN victims. And they saw this kid just happily minding his own business. Blood was dripping from Wolf's metal teeth as he sprang forwards. The speed and power of Wolf was truly amazing! The boy was slightly not to say totally helpless! He was completely in Wolf's power and —

Tid stopped to sort out all the red Smarties. He put them in a neat pile so he could eat them next. He'd just eaten one and typed in *Wolf's silver teeth sparkled in the moonlight,* when Danny came into the bedroom.

Nico came slouching in after him.

"Sure your mum's not in?" asked Nico, looking around as if Danny's mum might leap out of the wardrobe.

"No, I told you, she's at work until five o'clock."

"Get lost," said Danny to Tid, jerking his thumb at the door. "Me and Nico got serious stuff to talk about."

Tid gave a loud, huffy sigh and raised his eyebrows. But he scooped up his sweets and trudged out the door.

"What's that he's doing?" said Nico, peering at the computer screen.

"Oh, just one of his stories," said Danny. He clicked the mouse over "Exit" and Tid's Wolf story vanished from the screen.

"OK then," said Danny. "This is The Plan, right?"

He started to giggle. He just couldn't help it. All day at school, every time he'd thought about The Plan his face had cracked into a big grin. "Just what is so entertaining about my maths lesson?" Mr Walker had asked him in a dangerous voice. And Danny had truthfully said, "Nothing, sir," and hidden the grin behind his hand.

But now his laughter just exploded.

For sixty seconds he and Nico staggered about, cackling like drunken witches and aiming feeble punches at each other.

Then Danny said in a weak, gasping voice, "Right, Nico, stop messing about. We got to be serious."

Nico dragged a hand down over his face and like magic a new face emerged. It was glum as an undertaker's.

"OK," said Nico. "I'm serious now."

"We got to get this right," said Danny. "The Plan is I'm supposed to have found this new friend. Right? And he's, like, a *good* influence. He's like a saint or something. He never does anything wrong. So, part one of The Plan is, I tell Mum about this kid when she comes home and, hey presto, she stops worrying and gets all relaxed and forgets about the bad things and says, 'Oh Danny, I'm so thrilled you've found a decent friend at last, not like that frightful boy Nico —'"

Nico grinned and waggled his eyebrows up and down.

"—and then part two, you meet me at the phone box at six o'clock."

"What are we going to do then?" asked Nico.

"You'll see," said Danny mysteriously. "Just be there. Right?"

There was a scuffling noise outside the door. "Wait a minute," whispered Danny. "Shhh." He put his finger to his lips.

Then he leapt over to the door and threw it wide open, *crash*!

He checked up and down the landing.

"Tid, you there?" he shouted.

No reply.

"Nobody there," he said, puzzled. "I thought Tid was out there, listening."

He came back into the bedroom.

"Anyway, I'm off now," said Nico, looking anxiously out of the window. "I'll just nip over your backyard fence. Don't want to meet your mum coming down the road."

"Look, she likes you really," shrugged Danny. "It's just since we played truant. And the pancakes thing, you know tossing the pancakes. We shouldn't have done that. Why did we do that? That made her really mad."

"I dunno," puzzled Nico. "I can't remember why we did that. But I thought we cleaned up after ourselves pretty good."

"We forgot the ones stuck to the ceiling."

Nico shook his head and made a sad popping noise with his lips. Then he said, "Catch you later," and stomped off down the stairs.

Danny's head was buzzing with The Plan. He was thinking about what he was going to tell Mum. He was psyching himself up for it. So he didn't really notice when Tid stuck his head round the door and said, in a voice filled with doom:

"Wolf is coming to get you."

Chapter Five

"By the way, Mum," said Danny, "I've found a new friend."

His voice was casual. But he didn't feel casual inside. The Plan had to succeed. Then things would be like they were before. Back in those happy days when he had his freedom and Mum didn't cramp his style.

Immediately Mum was suspicious. You could practically see a pair of antennae on her head, waving about to detect lies.

"What's his name?" she demanded.

"Errr—" For a panicky second Danny's mind was a total blank. He'd thought of most things about his new saintly friend. But he hadn't thought of a name.

"Don't you even know his *name?*" asked Mum, narrowing her eyes.

It was a bad start. Danny had chosen this moment because usually his mum's defences were down. When she came home from work she was bone-weary with only enough energy to flop in a chair, slip off her shoes and sip a cup of tea. But now she was on the edge of her seat, quivering with attention.

Danny fished frantically in his mind. And came up with the name of a saint shot full of arrows.

"He's called Sebastian," he said, wincing as he said it.

But his mum approved of the name.

"Sebastian," she repeated. "That's a nice name. You don't hear that name often."

Danny was encouraged.

"Yeah, you'd really like him, Mum. He's a good kid. I've been listening to you, see, and I've chosen a good kid for a friend. He always does his homework and he's never been on detention and— "

"Does he go to your school?"

"Errr—" Danny's mind was racing. "Yes, he's in top band," he said.

"What do his mum and dad do?"

Danny's mind went into overdrive. He'd never

expected that question. What did she want to know that for?

"Err, I don't know," he said. "I've only just started hanging round with him. Kids don't ask each other things like that. But I'll find out if you like. Next time I see him."

"And where does he live?"

This was safer ground. Danny had prepared this answer. "You know that new posh estate?"

"You mean Elm Park?"

"Yeah, well, he lives there, in this great big house. That's good, isn't it?"

"I don't care if Sebastian lives in a big house or not," said Danny's mum, a shade too quickly, "so long as he doesn't get you into any trouble."

"Oh, he wouldn't," Danny assured her. "He goes to Sunday school and he never gave up piano lessons like I did, he's got Grade Four! And he gets Grade As at school and always does his homework. He even likes maths homework! And he doesn't get in any trouble. He always comes home on time and always tidies his room and always puts his dirty socks *in pairs* in the laundry basket and—"

Danny stopped. He could hear himself going way

over the top. Making Sebastian so perfect that Mum would be sure to smell a rat. So he balanced things up by saying, "And he's a really good laugh as well."

To his amazement, Mum believed in Saint Sebastian. "You can bring him round any time you like," she said. "I'd love to meet him."

"Errr – I don't know if his mum will let him. She doesn't like him to go far. She doesn't let him hang round the streets or anything."

"She sounds like a sensible woman," said Danny's mum. "Where did you say she works?"

Danny took a deep breath. "I didn't," he said.

This was getting complicated. He'd noticed before that lying always got complicated.

"Why can't she stop asking all these *questions*?" he thought as his brain whirred around. "Then I wouldn't have to tell her all these lies, would I?"

"Anyhow, got to go now," he gabbled at Mum. "I'm going round to Sebastian's now. Is that OK? I won't be back late."

"'Course it's OK," his mum said, without a trace of suspicion in her voice. "I'm really pleased you're mixing with a different crowd. Sebastian sounds like just the friend I'd have chosen for you."

"Sounds like a boring goody-goody prat to me," thought Danny as he trudged across the kitchen.

At the back door he hesitated. "*Erm*," he said, shuffling his feet. "Don't suppose I could have my cap back? Now I'm being good and everything?"

At first Mum pursed her lips and looked doubtful. Then she said, "I suppose it's OK."

She got the cap down from the top of the kitchen cupboards where she always hid things and gave it to him.

As he stepped outside the door, Danny gave a little private cheer, "Yay!"

He was really astonished to get the cap back. He almost hadn't asked. He'd thought there was no chance she'd say yes.

She wouldn't have said yes if it hadn't been for Saint Sebastian. "I've only just invented him," thought Danny gleefully. "And he's doing miracles already!"

He pulled the cap down on his head so it was a snug fit. He bent the peak into a sharper shape. It was a great cap. It felt like it had been made for him.

Tid came dashing round the side of the house and crashed into him. Danny was busy working out part two of The Plan. So he just cuffed his brother in an absent-minded sort of way and said, "Hey, you mong, where's the fire at?"

"Got to go," gasped Tid. "Wolf wants to see me. And he gets really mad if you're late."

"Wolf?" said Danny, vaguely. "Who's he? Is that his real name?"

"Dunno," said Tid. "That's what everybody calls him. I told you before, he says he's going to get you."

Danny laughed. "Oh, I'm scared, I'm scared," he warbled in a high, trembly voice. He laughed again. "Who is this Wolf then? Is he one of your weedy little mates?"

"Oh no," said Tid. "He's older than me. Older than you even. He's about sixteen, probably, and he's really strong. And when he says he's going to get you, you get got! Wolf doesn't mess about."

An icy spear touched Danny's heart. Just for a second. Then he laughed it off. "What am I supposed to have done then?"

Tid's voice became a fearful whisper. His eyes grew wide and scared. He looked over his shoulder, as if someone might be listening.

"You've made him mad," he said. "So you better keep out his way, Danny."

"How can I do that? I don't even know who he is!"

But Tid had already dashed away.

Danny stood still for a moment, his eyes clouded by uneasy thoughts. Then he shook his head and laughed.

"Stupid kid!" he said.

Chapter Six

"You got your cap back," said Nico as Danny strolled up to the telephone box. "How'd you do that?"

"It was Sebastian," said Danny. "He did it."

"Who?"

"This kid I made up. This goody-goody friend I'm supposed to have."

"His name's *Sebastian*?"

Danny shrugged apologetically: "Yeah."

"And does your mum really *believe* in him?" marvelled Nico.

"Yes," said Danny, as if he could hardly credit it himself.

Then he gave it some more thought. "But only

because she wants to so much. She's really worried about me, see. She thinks I'm turning out bad. And that it's all her fault." He made his voice spooky. "She thinks I'm on the slippery slope to *HELL*. So if I mix with someone like this Saint Sebastian, she thinks I'll sort of catch some of his goodness, like measles."

Nico rolled his eyes to Heaven. "Huh!" is all he said.

They crammed themselves inside the smelly telephone box.

"What we actually *doing* in here?" asked Nico, as Danny lifted the phone.

"You," said Danny, "are going to be Sebastian."

"Say that again."

"Just do what I tell you. Right?"

Danny put in a coin and punched in a phone number. It was the number of his own house. He listened down the line. *Brrr, brrr, brrr, brrr.*

"Come on, Mum," he said, into the phone. "I know you're in."

Tid picked up the phone. "Yep?"

"Is Mum there?"

"Who's that?"

"It's me, you idiot. It's Danny."

"Oh. Well, Wolf is still coming to get you. I just seen him tonight. He says he knows who you are."

"Will you shut up about this Wolf? Just get Mum. And get a move on."

Tiddler blew a giant raspberry down the phone and put it down. All Danny could hear was the television yakking away in the background.

"Come on, Mum, come on," he fretted.

Beep, beep, beep.

He had to ram in some more money. Then Mum came on the line.

"Hello, Danny? You're not in trouble, are you?"

"No, 'course not. I don't get in trouble now. I told you, everything's under control. I'm over here at Sebastian's house, you know in Elm Park?"

"Oh, right."

"Say hello to Mum, Sebastian," said Danny thrusting the receiver at Nico like a microphone.

Nico backed off as it was red hot. "Go on," mouthed Danny, nodding his head in encouragement.

Nico bent towards the phone. "Aw wight?" he grunted into it.

"No, no, no, no," stormed Danny, covering up the

mouthpiece. "Sebastian wouldn't talk like that. Say, 'Hello, how are you, Mrs Jackson?'"

"Hello, how are you, Mrs Jackson?" Nico mumbled stiffly as if his lips were frozen up from the dentist's. But it was OK. It was just what Danny wanted to hear. Because it didn't sound like Nico at all.

Danny slapped the phone back to his ear. "Did you hear him, Mum? That was Sebastian. Isn't he polite? He said hello, how are you?"

"Hello, Sebastian!" Mum called back down the phone. "How are you?"

Nico bent towards the phone again.

"That's enough," Danny whispered to him. He didn't want to push their luck.

"Anyway, Mum," he said down the line. "Me and Sebastian are working together on a homework project."

"What about?" asked Mum.

Danny cursed privately. His mum had a habit of pinning you down with tricky questions.

He clicked his fingers frantically at Nico. "Quick, quick, a project," he hissed out of the corner of his mouth.

"It's really hot in here," said Nico, pulling at the neck of his T-shirt.

"This project on – on global warming and it's really interesting and it's got to be in for tomorrow. So can I stay round at Sebastian's a little bit longer?"

Nico had started laughing. He had to crush his big hand over his mouth and he was doubled up, making terrible whooping sounds through his fingers.

"Shh! Shh!" warned Danny, who was listening for Mum's reply.

"Well, all right," she said. "So long as you're doing homework. What's that funny noise on the line?"

"Great! Thanks! Catch you later, little Mum!" said Danny, slamming down the phone before his mum had a chance to get suspicious.

They fell out of the phone box and rolled around on the grass, having hysterics.

"My stomach hurts," said Danny. "I got to stop laughing now."

He stopped and instantly his voice was deadly serious. He'd just remembered something he meant to ask Nico.

"Nico," he said, "do you know anyone round here called Wolf? Someone who's really tough, you know big and strong. Scary?"

Nico thought for a minute. Then he frowned and

shook his head. "What estate does he live on? What school does he go to?"

Danny shrugged. "Never mind," he said. "It's not important."

Later, he and Nico split up outside the pizza place. It was dark and Danny had to walk home on his own. He pulled his cap right down so he was hard to recognize. And, he just couldn't help it, he peered fearfully into every alleyway, every dark pool of shadow. Just in case Wolf was waiting to leap out at him.

Chapter Seven

"Tid, you awake?" asked Danny.

He leaned over the side of the top bunk and lobbed one of his dirty socks into Tid's face.

"Phew, geroff! What a stink!"

Tid was awake.

"Tid?"

A sleepy, "Yeah?" came from the bottom bunk.

"Tid, where does this Wolf go? Where does he hang around?"

Danny had told himself that he wouldn't ask about Wolf. He'd told himself to ignore all Tid's stupid warnings. But he'd been thinking about Wolf ever since he woke up. He just couldn't help himself.

"You know the graveyard in Eagle Road? The one behind those iron railings with the falling-over gravestones?"

"Yes."

"Well, he hangs around there with his mates."

"Has he got a gang then?"

"Yes, they're the Wolf Boys."

"The Wolf Boys?" sneered Danny. "What kind of a name is that?"

"It's what they're called."

"Well, why don't I know about them? Why have I never heard of this Wolf?"

Even as he asked this, Danny knew there were lots of reasons why he might not have heard of Wolf. If someone didn't live in your neighbourhood, or they went to a different school or weren't the same age as you or hung round in different places, then you wouldn't know them, would you?

"But why is he after me? What have I done?"

This was the question that most tormented Danny. Someone was after him and he didn't know why. It made him feel totally helpless.

"What have I done?" he asked Tid again.

"I don't know," said Tid. "What you've done

doesn't matter. Wolf is after you, that's all. That's what matters. He says he's got his eyes on you."

And as he said this Tid shivered, even though he was warm and cosy in his duvet. He was thinking about the yellow eyes and metal teeth he'd described in his story, filed away in the computer.

Danny was shivering too. He told himself not to be stupid. He told himself, "Just forget it." But it was too late. He already had Wolf on the brain.

"What's he look like?" he asked. He couldn't see Tid. He could only hear a voice coming up from the bottom bunk. The voice sounded small and terrified.

"He's big and tough," said Tid. "You'll know him if you see him. He's bigger than Nico."

"Bigger than Nico?"

Danny's stomach seemed to fall down a lift shaft. This was bad news. The worst possible news. "You mean he could beat Nico in a fight?"

Tid didn't answer. He just snorted, as if to say: "What a stupid question!"

"But what have I *done*!" yelled Danny desperately. "I don't even know what I'm supposed to have *done* to make him so mad!"

He didn't expect an answer. Tid had already said he

didn't know. So he decided to ask a more sensible question.

"How do you know this Wolf?"

"I'm in his gang," was Tid's amazing answer.

Danny thought he hadn't heard right. "What did you say?"

"I'm in his gang," repeated Tid. His voice was a strange mixture of fear and pride. "Well, I'm not actually in it yet," he added. "I'm sort of – a mascot really. They call me Baby Gangsta. They let me run errands for them. They say I'll be a proper Wolf Boy one day. And I hear stuff – you know, stuff they're saying to each other. And that's how I heard they were after you."

Danny's brain was buzzing like a nest of wasps. He had a million questions to ask. Like, did they use my actual *name*? And, do they know that you're my brother? But for a minute, his horror at what Tid had just told him drove them right out of his mind.

"You're crazy, Tid! How did you get mixed up in all this mess? You should stay out of gangs like that. They're poison. Once you're in, they never let you out."

"I know," said Tid miserably from the bottom bunk. "I know that, *now*."

Danny dangled over the side of his bed, so he could look Tid right in the eye. But Tid had got up. He was shuffling towards the door wrapped in his duvet, like a giant cocoon.

"Where you going?" demanded Danny. "Come back here! I haven't finished talking to you yet!"

Tid didn't answer. But Danny could hear the bathroom door being locked.

Danny sighed. Tiddler had a whole library of books in the bathroom. He kept them in the laundry basket. Sometimes he stayed in there reading them for hours.

"What's he got himself mixed up in?" muttered Danny. And at that moment he was more scared for Tid than he was for himself.

He swung down from the top bunk. He began looking in all Tid's hiding places. He didn't think twice about it. He looked inside his pencil case, under his mattress, in the pockets of his jeans. He was looking for something, anything, that would give him more information about Wolf. But he found no clues.

When he went downstairs for breakfast, Tid was still locked in the bathroom. Danny hammered on the door as he passed, using both fists. But Tid just yelled, "Go away. I'm reading."

Danny didn't even think about telling his mum that Tid might be in big trouble. Mum had had enough worry lately. And Danny didn't want to see her upset again, just when things were settling down. Besides, even if he'd wanted to tell her, she didn't give him the chance. As soon as she saw him she said, "Why don't you invite Sebastian round this evening?"

"Who?" said Danny.

Then he remembered. He'd forgotten about Sebastian. And his mind had to make a great leap sideways from thinking about the wicked Wolf, to thinking about saintly Sebastian.

"I'll have to tidy up," said Mum. "I bet they've got a lovely house."

"Oh yes they have, lovely," said Danny, saying anything that came into his head.

"And where did you say Sebastian's mum works?"

Danny happened to be looking at some white daisies, in a vase on the kitchen windowsill.

"The flower shop," he said. "She probably owns it or something."

He could have kicked himself. Why did he say that?

He hadn't meant to give Mum any more

44

information about Sebastian and his family. He'd meant to keep it nicely vague. But it was too late now.

Mum was hot on the trail. "What, you mean the one on the High Street?"

"No," said Danny wildly. "The other one."

"I know, you mean the one in the shopping mall, the very expensive one. And what does your friend Sebastian like to eat? He can have his tea here if he wants."

"He can't!" cried Danny with growing panic. "He's practising his piano! He's tidying his bedroom! He likes his bedroom to be really neat. And anyway he's a fussy eater. There's loads of things he doesn't like. He doesn't like practically anything that *normal* kids like."

"Well, he must eat something."

"He eats," said Danny, plucking the most unlikely thing he could think of out of thin air, "he eats a lot of avocado soup. He practically lives on it."

"Oh dear. Can you get that at the supermarket? What else does he like?"

"Got to go!" cried Danny desperately. "Late for school!"

"So you'll invite Sebastian round tonight? I'm

looking forward to meeting him. He sounded like a nice, polite boy on the phone."

Danny didn't answer. He didn't dare. Everything he said seemed to make the situation stickier. So he just grabbed his school bag and his cap and an ice-pop and slammed his way out of the house.

Danny's mum started to tidy up. She told herself, "It's not the Lord Mayor. It's only one of Danny's mates."

But she couldn't help feeling a tiny bit nervous about Sebastian's visit. She wanted to make a good impression on this new friend. Nico wouldn't notice if the house looked like a rubbish tip. But Sebastian sounded like a boy with high standards. The sort of boy who'd run his finger along furniture and go "Tut tut" at the dust.

"Don't be silly," said Danny's mum to herself. "He wouldn't do that."

But she got out the furniture polish.

"I know," she thought, as she polished away, "I could pop into the florist's after work and ask his mum what else he likes to eat. Then we won't make any mistakes."

Danny had left the house way too early. It was

twenty minutes before he was due to meet Nico to walk to school. And during those twenty minutes he felt more lonely and vulnerable than he'd ever felt in his life. He was being hunted by Wolf and he didn't know why. He didn't even know what the hunter looked like.

He didn't walk along the main road. Instead he pulled his cap low down over his forehead. Then he dived along alleyways and scuttled down back streets. He kept close to walls. He was like a ghost sliding from dustbin to dustbin. Only the star on his cap glittered faintly in the shadows.

When he reached the end of Nico's road, Nico wasn't there. Danny looked at his watch.

"Ten minutes to go."

He was out in the open now where anyone could see him. He remembered what Tid had said, "Wolf's got his eyes on you!"

Cringing, he looked around. But he didn't see anything to alarm him. There was a tiny kid on a yellow bike. There was a dog that looked like a mop on legs. There was no wolf.

"Maybe he's hiding," thought Danny. "And watching me."

For a second he had the crazy notion of leaping behind a tree and hiding there until Nico turned up. But he couldn't allow himself to do that. His pride wouldn't let him.

So he stayed out in the open. To anyone passing by he looked just like a normal kid, hanging around on a street corner. They couldn't guess how twitchy he was inside.

He was really pleased to see Nico come plodding up the street.

"Hey, Nico!"

There was something reassuring about having a friend like Nico. He was so big he looked like an earthquake couldn't shift him. While he was around you felt safe from the wolves.

Except that Danny remembered what Tid had said that morning: "Wolf is bigger than Nico," he'd said.

And, suddenly, Danny didn't feel safe at all.

Chapter Eight

Tid always got home from school half an hour before Mum got home from work. He unzipped his inside coat pocket, took out his key and let himself into the house. He grabbed a handful of chocolate chip cookies. Then went straight upstairs and switched on the computer. He was going to add a bit to his Wolf story.

Wolf doesn't know who I am, wrote Tid, typing feverishly and munching at the same time. *He doesn't know I'm Danny's brother. Last night he smiled at me with his silver teeth and yellow eyes and he said, "You're a good kid. I'm going to make you a Wolf Boy soon."*

And all his Wolf mates said, "Tid's all right!" But when Wolf is smiling you're more scared of him than when he isn't. I heard them talking. I was supposed to be running to the shop to get Wolf a new lighter. But I hid behind a gravestone and Wolf said, "Once you're a Wolf Boy, you're a Wolf Boy for life!" But I don't want to be a Wolf Boy any more. I don't like them any more. They scare me. But you can't escape from Wolf. Once he's got you, you're in his power for EVER and EVER and EVER and—

Tid closed his eyes and let his head droop forwards. He sighed. It was a sigh of deep despair.

He stayed like that for a long time. Then he opened his eyes again, slid off the chair and headed for the bathroom. He locked himself in, sat on the toilet and pulled the laundry basket towards him. He opened it and chose a book from his library. He was going to be there for some time.

In the empty bedroom the eerie green letters of his Wolf story were still glowing on the screen.

In the shopping mall, Danny's mum had just gone into the florist's. She scurried behind a vase of tall blue delphiniums and peered out.

She had just spotted Sebastian's mum serving a customer.

"That must be her," thought Danny's mum.

The other shop assistant was a young girl. She was looking suspiciously at Danny's mum. Danny's mum ducked behind a display of white waxy lilies – the kind people send to funerals.

Sebastian's mum looked just like Danny's mum expected. She was really smart. She had perfect hair and perfect clothes. Danny's mum looked down at her own jeans and trainers. She rubbed a hand over her spiky hair. She sighed.

"Don't be silly," she told herself. "She's not the *Queen* Mother or anything. And you only want to ask her what Sebastian likes for tea."

She checked her watch.

"I'm going to be late home," she thought. "Tid will be wondering where I am."

At last Sebastian's mum finished serving the customer. Her sharp eyes spotted Danny's mum lurking among the lilies.

"May I help you, madam?" she asked, gliding swiftly across the shop. And Danny's mum had to shuffle out from her hiding place.

Meanwhile, Tid was still reading on the toilet. All the books in his laundry basket library were like old friends. Some he'd had since he was a baby. He was reading one of those baby books now. It was tatty and torn and crusty with egg and banana. He wouldn't be seen dead reading it in public. But it soothed him in his distress. Like having a comfort blanket again.

As Tid read his book, Danny and Nico were strolling home from school.

"Two cows in a field," said Nico. "One says, 'Moo.' And the other one says, 'I was going to say that.'"

"Or," said Nico, "what about the two fish in a tank? One says, 'How do you drive this thing?'"

But Danny wasn't listening. He'd made a sudden decision.

"Let's go down Eagle Road for a change."

"What for? We never go that way. It's the long way round."

"I know. But there's something there I got to check."

"Fine," shrugged Nico.

The nearer they got to Eagle Road the more Danny felt his stomach scrunch up. Until it seemed as tightly clenched as a fist.

"What are we here for?" asked Nico, looking around. "This isn't our part of town."

"I told you I got to check something," insisted Danny. "It's about this Wolf. Tid says the graveyard in Eagle Road is where he hangs around."

"So what are we here for?" repeated Nico. "I thought he was going to get you? Best to keep out of his way."

"I know," said Danny. "But I think Tid's in a lot of trouble. I don't think he can handle it. He told me this morning, he's in this Wolf's gang. They call themselves the Wolf Boys. I just want to peek into this graveyard place. Not go in there or anything. Just see how many there are. See if Tid's in there with them."

"They're probably all just little kids," said Nico, shrugging. "Just messing around in a graveyard. Pretending to be tough. Scaring themselves stupid."

Nothing seemed to worry Nico. Nothing got him angry or upset. Danny wished he could be like that.

"Wolf isn't a little kid," he told Nico. "Tid says he really *is* tough. Wolf doesn't mess around."

They turned into Eagle Road. The railings of the graveyard were like a row of iron spears.

"We're just going to peek," warned Danny.

Sweat was prickling under his arms. What if Wolf had look-outs? What if they'd already been spotted? He tugged his cap low down on his forehead.

"What am I doing here?" he thought. "I'm checking up on Tid," he reminded himself. It had seemed like a good idea half an hour ago.

Now he wanted to run, bolt like a deer. But his pride wouldn't let him.

The railings started to unroll beside him. Nico poked his face between two of them.

"Careful," warned Danny. "Wolf might see you."

"There's nobody there," said Nico.

"You sure?"

"Yep. Look for yourself."

Danny took a quick sideways glance through the railings. He saw long grass, green shadows, gravestones toppled over. The place smelled of mould. You got a whiff of it even outside the railings. But there was no one there. No sound except some birds twittering. It was really peaceful.

"He'll probably show up later," said Nico. "He's probably gone home to have his tea."

The idea of Wolf having his tea made Danny laugh. He laughed and laughed because he was so relieved that, wherever Wolf was, he wasn't here now, in the graveyard.

"What's so funny?" asked Nico, thumping Danny on the back.

Danny straightened up, coughing.

"Look at the time," he said. "Better call Mum. There's a phone box at the end of the road."

Back at Danny's house, Danny's mum came staggering through the door with a huge bunch of white lilies. She dumped them on the hall table and went racing up the stairs. The bathroom door was locked.

"Tid, are you in there?"

"Just let me finish this chapter," came a faint voice through the door. "I've got to a good bit."

"Let me in, I'm desperate."

Brrr, brrr. The phone was ringing downstairs.

Danny's mum went racing down the stairs again and snatched up the phone.

"It's me, Mum."

"Danny? Where are you? You should be home by now."

"I'm at Sebastian's. We're doing our project. Say hello to Mum, Sebastian."

He held out the phone and Nico, right on cue, trilled, "Hello there, Mrs Jackson!"

Danny stuck up his right thumb and grinned.

"So you're not bringing Sebastian to tea tonight?"

"Can't, Mum. Not tonight. We're really busy."

Danny's mum said, "That's a pity." But what she really meant was, "Thank goodness." She hadn't spoken to Sebastian's mum in the florist's. At the last moment she'd chickened out and bought a large and very expensive bunch of funeral lilies instead.

"So I'll be back later, OK?"

Danny almost put the phone straight down. He took it for granted that his mum would approve. That Sebastian would work another miracle.

But instead his mum said, "Wait a minute. Where did you say you're calling from? Where does Sebastian live?"

"Err, err—" Danny glanced out of the phone box. There was a big black and white road sign right in front of him.

"Eagle Road," he said.

"I thought you said Elm Park?"

"Did I?" Danny had forgotten the first rule of lying – that you have to have a good memory. "Oh, you mong, Danny!" he thought.

"Did I?" he said again, playing for time. "Well, I made a mistake. And they both begin with 'E' don't they? No, Sebastian lives in Eagle Road, opposite the cemetery."

"Oh right," said Mum. But her voice sounded doubtful.

"Cheer up, little Mum. Don't worry about it! Everything's under control! At least you don't have to make no avocado sandwiches."

"I thought you said avocado soup?"

"Bye!" said Danny, before he could make any more mistakes. "Catch you later. Say bye bye, Sebastian." And he handed the phone to Nico.

"Woof, woof," barked Nico, into the phone.

Danny snatched the phone back.

"That was Sebastian's pet dog, Mum. She's called Poopsie. Say hello to Mum, Poopsie," he said shaking a threatening fist at Nico.

"Woof, woof!"

"Bye Mum!"

"Wait a minute," said Mum. "Weren't you supposed to hand in that project about global warming today?"

But Danny had already crashed the phone down.

"Phew!" he told Nico, slapping a hand against his forehead. "That was a near thing. But it was OK. I think I got away with it. You idiot, what did you bark like that for?"

"I just wanted to see what you'd do," grinned Nico. "Poopsie! That's the stupidest dog's name I've ever heard!"

"Yes, well, I didn't have much time to think did I? And there's a poster over there about pooper-scooping after your dog—"

"What kind of a dog is Sebastian's Poopsie?" interrupted Nico. He sounded really interested.

"Not you as well!" bawled Danny. "Asking me all these stupid questions about Sebastian. Look, this Sebastian kid, I *invented* him. Right? Just to get my mum off my back and make her stop worrying. He's not *real* you know. He doesn't actually *exist*."

"I know that. But what kind of a dog has he got?" insisted Nico.

"Oh, for Heaven's sake. One of those snappy little dogs with goggly eyes."

"My auntie's got one of those," said Nico. "It's disgusting. It slobbers all over you. Does Poopsie do that?"

58

Danny couldn't trust himself to speak. He just gave a great desperate howl "*AAAAARGH!*" of exasperation.

Back in Danny's house, Danny's mum was standing by the phone deep in thought. If she'd had antennae on her head they would be quivering. She hesitated. Then made a decision. She held the phone to her ear and punched in another number. Then she listened. What she heard at the other end of the line made her eyes widen in surprise.

"You know," Danny told Nico, as they walked away from the phone box in Eagle Road, "I got to write all this stuff about Sebastian down – where he lives, what his mum does, what he likes to eat, all that sort of stuff. Because it's getting a bit complicated. In fact I think I'll start now else I'll forget."

He rummaged around in his pocket and found an old stub of pencil. He found a screwed-up piece of paper. He smoothed it out.

"Stop a minute," he said to Nico.

He leaned the paper on Nico's back and began to write: "Sebastian likes: doing maths homework, tidying his room, practising his piano, helping his mum, being polite, avocado soup — Hey, I know quite a lot about him!"

Nico peered over his shoulder. "Avocado soup?" he queried.

"Yep," said Danny, still scribbling away in wobbly writing. "He's a really *weird* kid, this Sebastian."

Upstairs in Danny's house, the toilet flushed and the bathroom door was unlocked. Tid had finally reached the end of his book.

"Going out," Tid said to his mum as he passed her on the stairs. "Just over the football field."

"Be back for tea," she said automatically.

Tid gave her his mock salute. "Yes sir, Space Commander, sir!" But he wasn't grinning like he usually did. His face looked pale and strained.

His mum didn't notice. She was worried too. She was worrying about Danny's new friend, Sebastian.

Chapter Nine

Danny let himself into the kitchen. He tugged off his cap and was about to skim it on to the kitchen table, like he always did. But this time there was an obstacle in the way. It was a vaseful of giant white lilies.

"Where'd they come from?" thought Danny.

"Did you have a good time at Sebastian's?" asked Mum, coming into the kitchen.

"Er, yep," said Danny, warily.

He braced himself for a whole load of questions – about Sebastian's mum, his dad, his house in Eagle Road, his pet dog Poopsie. But his mum just said, "Tid hasn't come home yet."

"He'll be in trouble when he does get back," said

Danny's mum. "He came back for his tea then he rushed out again. And he should have been back half an hour ago."

The lilies had a strong, sickly scent. It made Danny think of funerals and graveyards. It made him think of the graveyard in Eagle Road, where he guessed Tid was right now, with Wolf and the Wolf Boys.

But he said to his mum, in his brightest, chirpiest voice, "Don't worry about it, little Mum! You worry too much! He's probably just playing football and forgotten the time."

Danny went up to the bedroom.

But he was restless. He lay on his bed reading a computer magazine. But he was listening all the time for the slam of the back door. Then he would know that Tid had come home safe.

"Who does this Wolf think he is?" Danny was thinking. "He wants to get me, only I don't know why. He's got Tid scared half to death. Who does he think he is?"

He went over to pull his bedroom curtains. And he couldn't help checking outside. Just in case Wolf was watching the house. But the road was empty.

On the way back to his bed he saw the computer screen flickering with words.

"Why doesn't Tid ever file things away?" he thought.

And he was just clicking the mouse over "Close" when the word "Wolf" sprang at him off the screen.

So he sat down on the swivel chair and began to read.

And as he read the expression on his face changed. First it was grim. Then he read, "Once upon a time". Then it was puzzled. And he read "silver teeth" and "yellow eyes", and then it was amazed and angry and relieved all at the same time.

"That little rat," he whispered to himself. "He's made it all up. It's only a story! He invented Wolf. Just like I invented Sebastian."

And Wolf was about as believable as Sebastian. "'Silver teeth and yellow eyes'," mocked Danny, shaking his head. "'Blood dripping from his teeth'! I'll kill him!"

He meant Tid not Wolf. He didn't believe in Wolf any more. Wolf was a story book monster. A bogeyman out of a kid's bad dream.

"And you fell for it," Danny sneered at himself. "I can't believe you fell for it."

He heard the back door slam. "I'll kill him!" he

cried, leaping up out of the chair. "Wait until I get my hands on him."

But he didn't get the chance. As if he knew he was in deep trouble, Tid scurried upstairs and locked himself in the bathroom.

Danny hammered a furious tattoo on the door. "Come out. I want a word with you! I want an explanation!"

He hammered and hammered until his mother yelled, "What are you trying to do? Break that door down?"

Danny gave a last disgusted kick at the door. Then went back into his bedroom. He deleted Tid's Wolf story.

"That's the end of him!" he said when there was a blank screen. It made him feel a lot better.

Chapter Ten

The next morning, Danny still hadn't managed to get his hands on Tid. He tried to stay awake but by the time Tid let himself out of the bathroom Danny was in a deep sleep. And this time, in his dreams, there were no wolves hunting him down.

When he woke up, Tid was just a lump under his duvet. He was still asleep, or pretending to be. Danny gave the duvet a couple of token kicks. "I want to talk to you!"

The lump didn't stir. But Danny was in a mellow mood. Now he wasn't scared all the time he could even appreciate the funny side of it.

"He nearly beat you at your own game," he

thought. "But I'm better. I'm class at inventing people. I never really believed in Wolf. But Mum believes in Saint Sebastian. She believes everything I say about him!"

And he went whistling down the stairs.

Mum was in the kitchen.

"After you phoned me last night I phoned the recall number," she said. "And you weren't phoning me from Sebastian's house at all, were you? You were phoning from a public call box."

Danny stopped whistling. "Danger, danger, danger!" his brain screamed at him.

"Err," he said. "Errrr."

"Don't tell me any lies," warned his mum.

Danny laughed in a light-hearted way. He put on his most casual voice. "So?" he shrugged. "It's not a *crime* is it? Me and Sebastian just went for a walk – with Poopsie. We just needed a break from doing all that homework. That's all. It's not against the *law*, is it?"

Mum chewed her lip. She didn't ask any more questions. But she didn't look satisfied either.

Danny didn't notice. He was too busy congratulating himself. "Brilliant!" he was thinking as he munched his toast. "You got out of that one OK. No trouble!"

He felt really confident and carefree this morning. As if nothing could go wrong.

He grabbed his cap and school bag. There were no blue ice-pops left! But even that didn't bother him. He just took a red one instead. Today nothing was going to spoil his good mood. He flung a breezy, "Catch you later," at Mum and swung out of the house.

He walked down the main road, crunching red ice. He didn't pull his cap down low. Or look over his shoulder or scuttle crab-like into alleyways. He didn't need to. Because he wasn't scared of Wolf any more. Wolf didn't exist. Not even on a computer screen.

When he heard Danny slam the door Tid crawled out from under his duvet.

"Are you still in bed?" yelled Mum from downstairs. "Hurry up, you'll be late for school!"

Tid locked himself in the bathroom. But he didn't open the laundry basket and take a book out of his library. Instead he checked in the mirror. He was looking at his neck. On his neck were four angry red marks. Tid put his hand up to touch one of them and winced. They hurt a lot.

When he went down to breakfast he had a red scarf wrapped round his neck. He hadn't worn a scarf since he was a little kid.

"What are you wearing that for?" his mum asked. "Scarves are for winter."

Tid bent his head over his cornflakes and said nothing.

"What's wrong with you this morning?" asked Mum.

Still Tid was silent.

Danny stood on the street corner waiting for Nico. He held his head high. The silver star on his cap flashed in the early morning sun. It shimmered every colour of the rainbow.

What was that?

Out of the corner of his eye Danny saw something move – in the shadows of the trees across the road. It was too big to be a dog. Far too big. He squinted, trying to make it out. It looked like someone crouching there—

"Hey, Danny," said Nico, slapping him on the back.

Danny leapt into the air.

"What's wrong with you?" laughed Nico. "You look like you saw a ghost!"

"Oh nothing, nothing."

And there was nothing wrong. Because when he checked across the road there was no one there at all.

"Don't be so jumpy!" he mocked himself.

"It wasn't that Wolf was it?" asked Nico, staring in the same direction as Danny. "Did you see him? Where is he?"

"He's nowhere," said Danny. "We don't have to worry about Wolf any more. He doesn't exist."

"What?"

"Tid made him up."

"You're kidding me!"

"No, I swear it. I found a story about Wolf on his computer. It was unbelievable! I mean, the guy in it had silver teeth and yellow eyes. He was like some monster out of a crap horror film."

"But what about the Wolf Boys and the graveyard at Eagle Road and Wolf coming to get you and everything?"

Danny shrugged: "All part of the story."

"The little rat!" said Nico, amazed and impressed.

"Yeah," agreed Danny. "That's what I said. But I never really believed him."

"What did he do it for?" asked Nico.

Danny shrugged again. But it had been bothering him as well – why Tid did it.

"I don't know. Maybe he wanted to get back at me for something. Maybe he just did it for a laugh—"

And he laughed himself, "Ha, ha, ha!" just to show Nico he treated it all as a big joke. He could never admit, even to himself, how real Wolf had been to him. How he'd looked for him round every corner. How he'd even had nightmares about him.

"Hey," said Nico, "you remember that time we talked about Sebastian? And you thought Tid was listening at the door? Maybe Tid thought, if Danny can go round inventing people, then I can too. Only he invented someone big and scary. He invented Wolf."

"That must be it!" said Danny, relieved there was some kind of explanation. "I'd forgotten about that. But if he was listening, he'd better not tell Mum about Sebastian. 'Cos the little creep's life won't be worth living if he does."

But Danny's mum didn't need telling about Sebastian. As soon as Tid had plodded out the door with the red woolly scarf round his neck, she galloped up the stairs.

"I hate doing this," she told herself, as she started searching for evidence.

She hit gold first time. In Danny's jeans pocket there was a piece of paper. She smoothed it out. It read like a profile of the saintly Sebastian.

"Likes tidying his room, likes practising the piano and being polite," read Danny's mum, her eyes slits of suspicion. "What's going on?"

There was a pillow on the bedroom floor. Danny's mum felt inside the cover and her fingers hit cold metal.

She pulled out what was inside. It was a massive hammer. A wicked, ugly-looking claw hammer, with a wooden handle, with tape wrapped round it.

"Oh no," said Danny's mum to herself. "What's Danny got mixed up in now?"

She looked from the claw hammer to the piece of paper. She'd been having more and more doubts about Danny's new friend. But now she was a hundred per cent sure that she'd been conned.

"I thought he was too good to be true!" she fumed. "All this rubbish," and she gave the piece of paper an angry shake, "about putting his socks in the laundry basket and tidying his room. Danny made all this up."

She couldn't imagine how she had believed it.

"I bet they planned this together," she thought. "All this stuff about what a wonderful boy Sebastian is. Probably thought it was a really good joke. But I bet Sebastian is even worse than Nico. I bet he's a really bad influence. And Danny is so easily led. Heaven knows what trouble this Sebastian is getting him into."

Then another thought hit her. "I wonder if Sebastian's mum knows what's going on? Mrs High and Mighty in the florist's? I think it's about time she and I had a little talk about her son!"

And with a fierce and gritty look in her eyes and the claw hammer in her handbag, Danny's mum set out for the shopping mall.

Chapter Eleven

While Danny's mum was speeding in her car to the shopping mall, Danny and Nico were strolling to school. Danny saw no more dark shapes crouching in corners. The world was a bright and sunny place, now that Wolf wasn't part of it any more.

Wolf had been like a great goblin squatting on his back, crushing him. Now the goblin had fallen off and rolled away. Danny felt he could breathe again. He felt as light as air.

If it hadn't been deeply uncool he would have skipped along the street like little kids do.

Instead he gave Nico a friendly cuff on the shoulder. "What's French for dentures?" he asked him. Then added, "It was a joke on a lolly stick."

"*Apéritif*," answered Nico, automatically. "I read that lolly stick too."

But Nico wasn't really paying attention. He was gazing across the road, into a pool of shadow by some wheelie bins.

"What you looking at?" asked Danny. He could see some kind of fluttering. For a second, his heart tightened.

Then Nico went darting across the road.

"It's a bird," Nico called back. "It's hurt itself."

"Relax," Danny calmed himself down. "Relax. It's only a bird."

He followed Nico across the road.

Nico was kneeling down on the pavement. "It's a seagull," he said.

They were miles from the sea. But there were lots of seagulls in town. They squawked on roofs and flew in white clouds round the Council rubbish tip.

"It's broken its wing," said Nico.

"Ugh," said Danny, "what's that red stuff hanging out?"

Feeling squeamish, he backed away. The bird was badly injured. One wing was ripped so tendons and bone were showing. The wing was useless. It spread out like a white fan on the pavement.

"We'll have to pick it up," said Nico.

Danny felt his stomach heave. He wanted to help the bird. He really did. But he didn't know what to do. It was in such a mess.

"What if we hurt it?" he said.

He couldn't bear to look at it. Let alone touch it. Just the thought of it made him squirm.

"Come on," he said to Nico. "Leave it. Someone else'll find it. We'll be late for school."

The bird tried to shuffle away. It looked nearly dead. Its broken wing dragged behind it. The white feathers were clogged with dirt.

But its eyes were still horribly alive. They were bright and black and hopeful. And Danny thought they were looking straight at him, pleading, "Do something."

"Come on, Nico," begged Danny, frantic to get away from those accusing eyes.

He pulled urgently at Nico's backpack. "Just leave it, Nico. OK? Don't try to pick it up. You'll hurt it."

But Nico stayed calm. "It's already hurt," he explained, patiently. "And I might be able to fix it. I fixed a blackbird's wing once. My grandad showed me how."

Nico took off his jacket. Gently, he scooped the bird up and wrapped it in the jacket so it wouldn't struggle.

"Can you really save it?" asked Danny.

Now the bird was wrapped up and he couldn't see the dreadful wound, he came closer again. "Can you make it fly again?"

"Don't know," said Nico, shaking his head. "Wings are tricky things to fix."

Danny felt ashamed of himself because he'd got in a panic. "I didn't want to hurt it," he said, desperate to explain.

Nico just nodded. He didn't seem to blame Danny at all. "You go to school," he said. "I'll see to this. I'll catch you later."

"OK," said Danny, gratefully.

Danny watched him walk off, carrying the bird like a precious parcel. He felt very proud of Nico.

"Didn't know he could fix birds' wings," he thought. Nico was full of surprises.

And he wished with all his heart that his mum could have seen Nico with the seagull. How he'd kept his head. How he'd known just what to do. How gentle he'd been.

"She wouldn't think he was a yob," thought Danny. "She'd really like him. If she'd seen him just now." He was thinking about all these things as he walked to school. He was wondering if the bird would survive. So at first he didn't take in what was painted on the wall slap-bang in front of him.

Then he focused on it. And leapt back. WOLF was written in big, red letters on the wall. And beneath each letter red paint was dripping, like blood.

Chapter Twelve

Danny's mum marched into the florist's like she was going to war. She was going to tackle Sebastian's mum. And nothing was going to stop her.

"And, this time don't buy any of her darned flowers," Danny's mum warned herself.

The claw hammer felt heavy in her bag. She had brought it along as evidence. She didn't exactly know what Sebastian and Danny were going to use it for. But she was convinced they were up to no good.

The smart woman was arranging a bowlful of pink carnations.

She looked up as the door crashed shut behind Danny's mum.

"May I help you, madam?"

Danny's mum strode across the shop: "I'd like to have a word with you about your son, Sebastian."

"Excuse me?"

"I'm Danny's mum," explained Danny's mum, tapping her foot impatiently.

The smart woman's face didn't light up with understanding. Instead it creased into a puzzled frown.

"I haven't got a son—" she began.

But Danny's mum was in no mood for listening. She was all fired up. She was determined to speak her mind.

"I thought at first that your son Sebastian was a perfect friend for my Danny. Danny told me all sorts of lies about him. What a fool I was! It was all a total invention, wasn't it? To put me off the scent. Doing homework! Ha! Tidying his room! Putting his dirty socks in the washing! Practising the piano! I should have known better. But the pair of them pulled the wool right over my eyes."

"I haven't got a—"

The smart woman was about to say, "I haven't got a piano." But she was left flapping her mouth like a landed fish as Danny's mum ranted on.

"I'm not saying my Danny's a saint because he's not. But he's very easily led. And I'm certain your Sebastian is getting him into trouble. Look what I found hidden in Danny's pillowcase."

And she pulled the evidence out of her bag and waved it around.

The smart woman backed away.

"Tina," she called sharply to a white, scared face amongst the roses. "Call Security."

"What?" Danny's mum stopped raving and looked around.

"Security? What do we need them for? I'm talking about your son, Sebastian. Aren't you interested in what he's up to? Most mothers would be grateful."

"Tina!" snapped the smart woman, with her eye on the claw hammer.

Danny's mum dropped the hammer back into her bag: "Well, I can see I'm wasting my time. Sebastian has got you fooled too, hasn't he? You think he's little Mr Perfect, don't you? Well, let me tell you, it's all a total invention. And you're in for a very nasty shock!"

And she stalked towards the door.

She slammed it shut so hard behind her that all the flower petals trembled.

Tina crept from among the roses.

"Shall I call Security, Miss Pringle?"

"No, I don't think so Tina. It's all right. She's gone now."

Miss Pringle shook her head sadly. "What was she saying about her son? Poor woman, obviously driven half-mad with worry."

Danny's mum went rushing across the mall. She was very late for work. But she felt pleased with herself. She felt it had gone rather well.

"I told her a few home truths," she congratulated herself. Then she shook her head sadly. "Some parents," she thought, "they're totally blind. They can't see what's going on right under their noses."

Chapter Thirteen

At lunchtime, Danny waited anxiously for Nico by the drinks machine on the second floor landing. Nico didn't turn up.

Danny ripped the ring pull off his Coke and took a swig. He leaned against the wall, surrounded by pushing schoolkids, and thought about the seagull.

"Hope it's all right. If anyone can make it all right, Nico can."

He kept seeing the same thing in his head. Nico stooping down to help the bird while he cringed back, not knowing what to do. And he wished again that his mum could have seen it. It made him angry when she said bad things about Nico. When she said he wasn't a good enough friend.

"She doesn't know what she's talking about," thought Danny, taking another swig.

He also thought about the blood-red letters on the wall. He could see them in his mind: WOLF.

"Just a coincidence," he decided and shrugged.

"Hey, move!" someone yelled in his ear. Without hurrying, Danny shifted himself a few centimetres to the left.

He had another thought. "Maybe Tid painted it. Maybe it's part of his plan to make me think Wolf is real."

Then he told himself, "Naaa, Tid wouldn't go that far. It's coincidence, that's all."

And he dismissed the graffiti from his mind.

Brring! Brring!

That was the bell for the end of lunch. The crowd broke up as kids began to move to classrooms. Still Nico hadn't showed up.

Danny leaned over the railings and looked down. He saw a red fuzzy head coming up the stairs.

"Nico! Where you been?" he yelled, his voice bouncing around the stairwell.

Nico looked up and grinned. "I been getting told off. For being late. And before that I was fixing that seagull's wing."

"Did you fix it?"

Nico shrugged. "I made a splint like my grandad showed me. I taped it up. Have to wait now. Look at that!"

He held up his hand to Danny. The thumb had a red hole in it.

"It pecked me." Nico inspected the wound. He laughed. "It doesn't know I'm trying to help it. Have to wear gloves next time I go near it."

Brring! Brring!

That was the bell for the start of lessons.

"I'm going to be late again," said Nico, shaking his head. "I've got to go right over to the gym."

"See you then, Nico. See you at home time."

"See you."

And they plodded off in different directions.

At his school Tid was slumped in his chair. There was an excited buzz all around him. The teacher was giving out brightly-coloured paper and silver and gold foil and scissors and paints. They were doing a project on making masks. They had already looked at African masks and carnival masks and now they were making one of their own.

Along with everyone else, Tid started to cut and stick and paint. But he was thinking about something else.

"I'm going to be a Wolf Boy soon," he was thinking. "And then I'll never, ever escape."

He put a hand up to the scarf on his neck. Some kids had tried to tease him for wearing it. He'd screamed, "Get lost! Mind your own business!" And they'd run off, scared by the ugly expression on his face.

His hand crept underneath the scarf. "Ouch!" The red marks still hurt.

They were burn marks. They were part of the initiation rites you had to go through to be a Wolf Boy. Wolf tore the ring pull off a can and heated it up with his cigarette lighter. And held it on your neck. And you weren't supposed to yell or anything. You weren't supposed to show any pain.

As he made his mask, Tid thought about the claw hammer hidden in his pillowcase. He still had another part of his initiation to go through. He had to do it tonight. After school he had to go to Eagle Road and get his instructions from Wolf personally.

Tid shivered at the thought.

"That's very nice," someone said, above his head.

In a daze, Tid looked up. His teacher was leaning over him.

"That's a very nice mask, Jonathan," she said again. "We'll have to put that in our wall display."

Tid looked down at the desk. While he was thinking his hands had been busy. They had made a mask. It was a snarling wolf mask with yellow eyes and gleaming silver foil teeth.

After school Nico and Danny met by the school gate. The first thing Danny did was take his cap out of his school bag and pull it low over his head. You weren't allowed to wear caps inside school.

"That's a great cap," said Nico. "That silver star is class. Wish I could get one like it."

He reached out as if he was going to tweak the cap off Danny's head.

"Well you can't," said Danny, dodging away. "It's unique, this cap. It's my lucky cap. I was meant to find it."

They got to Nico's corner where they usually split up. But this time Nico said, "Want to come round our house and see the seagull? It's in the shed. I'm going to try and feed it some fish tonight."

"Do you think its wing'll mend?"

"If it won't eat, it don't matter if the wing mends or not. 'Cos it's going to die anyway."

Danny didn't want to think about the seagull dying. So he put another picture in his head. Even though they'd found it among dustbins, he pictured the gull out at sea, swooping through a blue sky, dipping along foamy waves.

"It won't really die, will it?" he asked Nico. "Not really?"

He could hear the pleading in his voice. Nico could hear it too. But he still didn't answer.

He just said, "Come and see it," as if it might be Danny's last chance.

Danny suddenly decided he couldn't face seeing the gull.

He told himself, "Don't be pathetic!" He was disgusted with himself for being so useless.

But he couldn't bear to look into bright, black eyes that might be dead eyes tomorrow.

He mumbled, "I'll come over later."

He pretended to check his watch, though the time

was just a blur. "Mum'll be home now. You know what she's like lately. She worries like crazy if I don't get home on time."

"Hey, want to phone up?" Nico suggested. "I can pretend to be Sebastian. I'll say, 'We're taking Poopsie for a walk, Mrs Jackson.' Then she'll stop worrying. And you can come and see the seagull."

"Better not use Sebastian too much," Danny blurted out. "She might get suspicious."

"OK," said Nico. "Catch you later."

And he breezed off down the street.

Danny stared after him. He knew that if Nico hadn't been there this morning the gull would be already dead.

"Because you'd have left it to die next to those dustbins, wouldn't you?" he accused himself. "You didn't even dare pick it up."

Danny started to walk, not towards home but just wandering, anywhere, through the streets.

WOLF.

Danny gasped. The name sprang out at him from the wall. He'd forgotten it was there.

Instantly, he felt those old familiar stomach cramps. He looked over his shoulder. Was someone hiding, like this morning, in the shadow of the trees across the road?

"For Heaven's sake," he lectured himself. "He's a story, remember. A little kid's story."

Wolf didn't exist any more. He'd been wiped off the computer. He didn't even exist in cyberspace.

"So how come you're still behaving like he's real?" Danny asked himself in his most sneery voice. He was double-disgusted with himself. First he was scared of a dying seagull. And now Tid's bogeyman.

"Stop creeping about!" he ordered himself savagely. "Stop being so jumpy! You'll be looking under your bed for monsters next. Listen, you don't have to go down backstreets any more. You can go anywhere in this town! You can even walk through the graveyard in Eagle Road."

And suddenly, it was as if he'd been given a challenge. A daring deed to make up for being useless about the gull.

In his heart, he knew it was a cheating challenge. Because, now Wolf didn't exist, there was nothing to be scared of, was there? But it still seemed really important to walk through the graveyard. To do it alone without Nico. And, in a weird way, Danny knew that would give him his pride back.

But first he had to phone his mum.

He stopped at a phone box: "Mum, that you?"

"Where are you, Danny? I got home from work and no one's here. Tid's not here."

"Don't worry about it. He's probably playing football or something."

"Will you stop telling me not to worry? It worries me when you do that! Where are you anyway?"

"I'm at Sebastian's, of course. Say hello to Mum, Sebastian."

Danny held out the phone. Then realized, with a sickening lurch of his stomach, that he was holding it out to empty air. Faithful Nico wasn't by his side. So he muffled his mouth with his hand and squeaked, "Hello, Mrs Jackson," into the phone.

On the other end of the line Danny's mum said, "What are you two up to? And don't tell me you're doing lots of maths."

Danny had to gulp back his next words. Which were going to be, "We're doing lots of maths."

"We're just taking Poopsie for a walk," he improvised.

"Pull the other one," said Danny's mum. "It's got bells on."

"Pardon, Mrs Jackson?" said Danny in his squeaky Sebastian voice. "What did you say?"

Beep, beep, beep.

"My money's run out," yelled Danny, just as Mum was about to say, "I've found the hammer—"

"Phew," thought Danny as he clashed the phone down. "She's in a funny mood tonight."

But he dismissed it from his mind. There was no accounting for his mum's moods. And, anyway, he was on a mission. He was going to walk through the graveyard in Eagle Road. With his head held high. Without once looking over his shoulder or giving in to fear.

"No fear," murmured Danny to himself. "No fear. Right?"

And, as he held his head up, the silver star on his cap flashed blue and green and orange, like the Northern lights.

Back home, Danny's mum also put down the phone. She scribbled a note for Tid.

"Back soon. Chocolate ice-cream in freezer. Love Mum."

Then she went out to the car. She was just opening the door when she had a thought. She dashed back into the house, got the claw hammer and flung it into the back seat.

"Evidence," she thought.

Then she scorched out of the drive. Danny's mum was always a careful driver. But this time she hurled the car round corners like a boy racer. She was going to Eagle Road. She didn't quite know what he was up to but she was convinced Danny was in bad company. She was going to rescue him. And put him back on the straight and narrow. Before his dad came home.

Chapter Fourteen

Tid wasn't playing football. Straight after school, he'd started out for Eagle Road to meet Wolf. He took off his scarf. He didn't want to be wearing a red woolly scarf when he met Wolf. And besides, you weren't supposed to hide your initiation marks. You were supposed to be proud of them. Because they meant you were a Wolf Boy.

Tid wasn't quite a Wolf Boy yet. He had one more test to pass. Tonight he had to take the claw hammer and smash the window of a car and steal something. Maybe a mobile phone or a radio. Then he had to take what he'd stolen plus some chunks of glass as evidence to Wolf. Then he would be a proper Wolf Boy.

Tid was thinking about what he had to do. His stomach felt trembly, as if it was full of butterflies with fast-beating wings. He wasn't watching where he was going. He bumped straight into Nico.

"Hey, Tid! So where you going?"

"So where *you* going?" mimicked Tid rudely. He was nearly a Wolf Boy now. And Wolf Boys didn't answer anybody's questions.

Nico wasn't offended. He just grinned. "I'm going home." He jerked his thumb down the street. "That's where I live."

Tid didn't say anything. But he was secretly sneering. He thought Nico was soft. He thought someone as big and strong as Nico should act tough and scary all the time, like Wolf did.

Nico looked down at the scowling Tid. His grin changed to a frown.

"What's that on your neck?" he said.

Part of Tid wanted to swagger. Part of him wanted to boast, "I'm a Wolf Boy now. I'm in Wolf's gang!"

Then Nico said, "They're burns, aren't they? From ring pulls? Who's been doing that to you?" He sounded really outraged.

And instead of swaggering, Tid burst into tears.

Nico crouched down so he was looking straight into Tid's tear-streaked face.

"Tell me," he said.

But Tid couldn't stop crying. Violent sobs were shaking his skinny body. For weeks now, he'd been scared to death. It had all started so casually. Someone he'd met playing football, a bigger boy, had taken him along to Eagle Road. And he'd run errands for the Wolf Boys. He'd been pleased to do it. Every time Wolf had taken notice of him he'd glowed with pride.

"Who did it?" insisted Nico gently. He took Tid's arm. "Who did it?"

Tid tried to fling the arm away. "Geroff, geroff, geroff!" he screamed. "None of your bloody business!"

But he couldn't break Nico's grip. Suddenly, he stopped struggling. He couldn't cry any more either. So he sniffed and hiccuped a bit. And then he was quiet.

"Who did it?" asked Nico, patiently. "I'm not going to let you go until you tell me."

"I got to go and meet Wolf!" cried Tid, frantically.

Nico looked really startled. "You mean, Wolf is *real*?" he asked Tid. "You talking about the Wolf who's after Danny? He's a *real* person? I thought you made him up."

" 'Course he's real!" cried Tid, squirming in Nico's grasp. "He's real as you or me. And I'm one of his Wolf Boys and if you don't let me go he'll beat you up. He'll kill you."

"And did this creep burn your neck with ring pulls?"

Tid stopped fighting. He started crying again. He couldn't help it. It was such a huge relief that someone knew what was happening to him. His mum didn't know. She was too worried about Danny. His dad was far away in another country. And it was no use asking Danny. Danny was top of Wolf's hit list.

Nico let go of Tid to scratch his head. It was hard to know what to make of all this. He still wasn't a hundred per cent sure that Wolf existed. It struck him that Tid might be playing some kind of private fantasy game. That he might even have made those marks himself.

Tid didn't run when Nico let him go. He just slumped against a wall. And he found himself telling Nico his deepest fears. Things he hadn't told anyone since he first went to Eagle Road.

"I got into his gang, see. And at first I thought it was

great, then I heard things about what they was doing. Bad things. They was robbing cars and houses and all sorts of other stuff that I can't tell you. I was dead scared but by then I knew too much and Wolf said a Wolf Boy never leaves the gang, he's in it for life. But I wanted to leave, it was scary, they made me do things I didn't want to do. Then I heard they was after Danny and I didn't dare say I was his brother and I was scared in case they found out and—"

Nico listened carefully to this jumble of words. Every so often Tid stopped to hiccup or sniff or wipe his nose on his sleeve. But by the time he'd finished Nico was almost convinced that Wolf wasn't just a fantasy. That he was real. And dangerous.

"—and I got to steal some stuff tonight," said Tid in a whisper. "I got to break into a car."

"Who says so?"

"Wolf says so. He gave me his own personal hammer to do it with."

"Where is it?"

"I hid it in my bedroom. It's too heavy to carry about. I got to go back for it later after I seen Wolf at the graveyard."

Nico was thinking hard. Suddenly he made a decision.

"You and me are going to see this Wolf," he said.

Tid got frantic again. He was almost mad with panic. "No you can't!" he cried. "He's tougher than you. There's nothing you can do. Nothing anyone can do. I can't escape. I'm nearly a Wolf Boy now."

Tid started to run. Nico tried to stop him but Tid twisted away and went haring down the street.

Nico stared after him. He sighed and shook his head. "Poor kid," he muttered.

He thought about the seagull. He should be home feeding it. But it would have to wait. Tid was more important.

He set off, with his slow plodding tread, to follow Tid to the graveyard.

Chapter Fifteen

Danny's mum wasn't making good progress. She was stuck at roadworks. As the cars crept forward she was fretting about what to do when she finally reached Eagle Road.

"I'll knock on doors," she decided. "Find out which is Sebastian's house. It can't be that difficult," she thought. "There can't be more than one kid called Sebastian with a mum who's a florist and a dog called Poopsie."

While his mum fumed in the traffic jam, Danny was already walking into Eagle Road. There had just been a shower. The pavements were slick and wet. The spears round the graveyard gleamed like silver. Danny could see broken gravestones inside the railings and a jungle of long, wet grass.

He didn't feel the buzz he expected, walking alone down Eagle Road. He felt very uneasy. It wasn't Wolf – he knew now that Wolf didn't exist. But it was the gloomy, dripping graveyard that spooked him.

"You're not scared of ghosts, are you?" he mocked himself. "Jumping up from behind gravestones and going 'Whoooo'!"

He laughed. But it was a forced, jittery laugh.

Still, it was too late now. He'd made himself a challenge so he had to do it. And to do it properly he had to walk right through the graveyard. Only that would make up for the seagull.

The iron gate squeaked as he pushed it open. He pulled the peak of his cap down. Then stepped inside.

It was like a time warp in here. So hushed and still. You couldn't even hear the cars in the road.

Kak, kak, kak, kak, kak.

Angry chattering burst the silence.

"What's that?" Danny's eyes looked round, wildly.

A magpie exploded out of a bush right in front of him.

Danny jumped like a frightened frog.

Kak, kak, kak.

He grinned, embarrassed. "It's just a bird," he told himself. "Will you calm down? There's nothing to be scared of. No fear! OK?"

And suddenly he felt bubbly with confidence.

He pushed his way through the grass. He felt great, a real world-beater. Like all the spooks in the world couldn't stop him now. "Come on you spooks!" he invited them, grinning like mad. "Come on you—"

Then he saw Wolf, sitting on a tombstone.

For a few seconds there was a great black hole in Danny's mind. And he could feel himself plunging down it. He could hear himself yelling "*Aaaaaargh!*" But no sound came out of his lips.

"You got my cap on," said Wolf.

Danny opened his mouth. Still no words came out.

His brain had collapsed into whirling confusion. His legs folded up. He sagged against a gravestone. But his eyes carried on working. And he saw that Wolf's top teeth glittered, as if they were made of metal. And that he had strange eyes. They were greeny-yellow, pale as lemons.

"Tid was right," Danny's shocked brain told him.

"He was right about the yellow eyes and silver teeth."

But Wolf was no horror story monster. Wolf was real. He was breathing. Danny could have reached out and touched him.

Wolf spoke again. And then Danny saw that the silver gleam was a brace, clamped on to his top teeth. That should have made Wolf less scary. But somehow it didn't.

"That's my cap," said Wolf again, even more softly this time.

Danny tried to pull his shattered brain together. "I found it," he said. "In the road."

"You should have given it back," said Wolf. "Everyone knows that's my cap. Only I'm allowed to wear it."

"I didn't know," said Danny.

Wolf ignored this. "You're asking for trouble," he said. "Wearing my cap. *Deliberately* wearing it."

He was big, maybe bigger than Nico, with a face that seemed frozen. It hardly moved when he spoke. There was no expression on it at all. Only his pale eyes flickered.

"My Wolf Boys been watching you," said Wolf. "And that mate of yours, that big ginger-nut. I thought, he must be crazy wearing my cap. Then I thought, maybe he's doing it, like, *deliberately*. Maybe it's some kind of challenge. Like he's saying, 'I'm the boss around here and not you.' Maybe he wants to take over. Maybe he wants to fight. So I said to my Wolf Boys, 'No, don't get him. Leave him to me.'"

Danny gulped. The idea that Wolf thought of him as a rival should have made him sick with fear. But instead a crazy thing happened. Deep in his muddled brain Danny felt quite flattered. It was like magic. He felt instantly tougher and braver. He felt as hard as nails.

Tid had arrived at the graveyard. He was hanging on to the railings looking in. The first thing he saw was the star in Danny's cap, shining among the gravestones. Then he saw Wolf.

"Oh no," he thought. "Wolf's got my brother. He's got Danny!"

He crouched down and poked his ear through the railings. He could just about hear what Wolf was saying.

Wolf sounded quite chatty. As if he was in a good mood. But Tid knew better. You never knew what Wolf would do next. That's what made him so scary. In a second he could change from sunshine to blackest storm.

"Run, Danny, run," whispered Tid as he clung to the railings.

But Danny didn't run.

Wolf said, "But I probably got it wrong. Because no one would challenge me. No one would be that stupid. So let's just say you're stupid, OK? So just give me the cap back. And I'll let you go, stupid."

Tid thought, "Phew. He's letting him go." He felt weak with relief. He thought, "Danny, you don't know how lucky you are."

He waited for Danny to take off the cap and hand it over. But instead Danny did an incredible, reckless thing. Tid couldn't believe his ears. His eyes grew wide with shock and horror.

"No," said Danny. "This is my cap now."

Tid didn't wait to hear the rest. He started to run towards the cemetery gates.

Behind him Nico shouted, "Tid, you wait there!"

But Tid didn't even hear him.

When Danny said no, Wolf's face didn't change.

He pretended to rake out his ears. "Say that again," he said. "I can't be hearing right."

Something was happening to Danny's boldness. A part of his brain was shrieking, "What are you doing, you fool?"

He tried to ignore it. "I found it," he said. "So it's my cap now."

He was half-aware of strange rustlings all around him. A bush quivered. Somewhere he thought he heard a laugh. But just as he was thinking, "There's someone else here!" there was a terrific crashing in the bushes. And Tid skidded to a halt beside him, panting.

"You leave my brother alone!" Tid gasped. "You let him go."

This time Wolf's face did change. It showed faint surprise.

"Well, well, well," he said. "Stupid and his stupid brother. And I nearly made you a Wolf Boy, Tid. I think you're a spy, Tid. I think you've been telling stupid here and his ginger-nut mate all our private business."

"No, I never, Wolf," gabbled Tid. "I never told them nothing."

Outside the railings Nico was sizing up the situation. And he saw how explosive it was. If he went in there it should have been three against one. They might have stood a chance. If it hadn't been for the Wolf Boys hiding in the long grass. Nico had counted three of them so far. But there could be more.

His brain was racing like mad, puzzling how to rescue Tid and Danny, when someone said, "Is that him then? Is that Sebastian?"

Nico whirled round. It was Danny's mum. He could see her car parked at the end of Eagle Road.

"Shhh, Mrs Jackson. He'll hear you."

"I don't care if he does hear me," said Danny's mum. "What's Tid doing in there? Is he mixed up in this too? What's going on? I'm going in there to give Sebastian a piece of my mind."

Nico groaned. "Please don't, Mrs Jackson. Please, please don't."

"Look," hissed Danny's mum. "Look what I found in Danny's pillowcase."

And she showed Nico the claw hammer.

Nico didn't say, "That was Tid's pillowcase." He didn't say, "That's Wolf in there, not Sebastian." There was no time for explanations. He could see one of the Wolf Boys sneaking through the long grass.

Time to make a move, he thought.

It was going to be tricky. He understood that Wolf

was very dangerous. But Danny's mum didn't. She thought she could rush in there like the cavalry. Tell Wolf off like a naughty schoolboy! He had to stop her. He took a deep breath.

"Mrs Jackson, I'm going to get Danny and Tid out of there. That Sebastian, he doesn't play games. He's serious trouble."

Danny's mum took a sharp, suspicious look at Nico. He was grim-faced. "What are you going to do?" she asked him.

"I don't know yet. Just try to stop things getting violent."

"Violent?" spluttered Danny's mum. "There'll be no violence here. If Sebastian lays a finger on my kids, I'll kill him!"

Nico groaned again and tugged at his fuzzy hair.

"Shhh, shhh, Mrs Jackson. I know you don't like me. But Danny's my best friend. I won't let nobody hurt him. So please let me sort this out. OK? You don't know what you're dealing with. Honest, you'll just make it worse."

He was scared he'd said too much and Danny's mum would get mad. But she didn't.

Instead she decided to trust him. Nico's words were

so heart-felt and desperate that she felt ashamed. She even started to say, "Look, Nico, it's not true I don't like you—"

Suddenly Wolf's voice roared out from inside the graveyard.

"Give me that hammer," said Nico urgently.

Danny's mum hesitated.

"It's all right," said Nico. "I'm not going to hurt no one with it."

Danny's mum handed it over.

"Catch you later, Mrs Jackson," Nico said.

He hid the claw hammer under his coat. Then walked through the cemetery gates.

Chapter Sixteen

Nico walked through the gravestones and long grass. He was aware of the Wolf Boys around him. They weren't hidden any more. They were out in the open now, watching the show. But he wasn't interested in them. They would only do what Wolf told them to.

He was near enough now to hear what Wolf was saying. "Don't you know who I am?" he was saying to Danny. "You a retard or something?" One of the Wolf Boys sniggered.

"If Wolf asks you to do something, you do it," said Wolf.

Nico knew that Wolf could get his cap back. He could take it off Danny any time he liked. But he was having fun, playing with Danny and Tid like a cat plays with a bird. Making them wait to find out what he was going to do with them.

"Your last chance," said Wolf, drumming his big boots on the tombstone. "Give it back." He was getting bored now. "Or else I'll have to give you a good kicking."

"No," said Danny.

There was a wild and stubborn look in his eyes. Even though his stomach was doing loop-the-loops.

"Give it to him," begged Tid. "What you doing? If you give it to him he'll let us go."

"No he won't," said Danny.

And Wolf grinned, a silver, wolfish grin. He could see that Danny was scared. He enjoyed scaring people.

Then he saw Nico. His stone face didn't show any surprise.

"Thought you'd be around," he said. "I'm just about to annihilate your mate here. He took my cap. He thought it would make him really hard if he wore it. As hard as me. That's a good joke, isn't it?"

And Danny saw, in a flash, that Wolf had never seriously thought of him as a rival. He was just amusing himself, having a good laugh at Danny's expense.

Then Danny felt his cap lifted off his head. He made a wild grab for it. But he was too late. Nico had got it.

Without hurrying, Nico fitted the cap on his own head. It was too small. He took it off and adjusted it. Then he pulled it on again.

"I've got your cap now," he told Wolf.

Danny should have been grateful. Wolf's eyes were on Nico. Not on him. Wolf would have to fight Nico now. But instead he was furious.

He jumped for the cap. "That's my cap!" But Nico ducked out the way. As he did, his coat flapped open and Wolf saw the claw hammer, tucked inside his belt.

Nico didn't once look at Danny. It was as if Danny wasn't there. He kept his eyes on Wolf.

"Let them go," he said to Wolf. "And tell your Wolf Boys to keep off."

Wolf pulled on his ear, as if he was thinking about this. He made them wait. And wait.

Then he gave a quick shrug. "OK," he said to Nico. "But you stay here."

"Get lost," said Nico to Danny and Tid. He still didn't look at them.

"No," said Danny.

"Please," begged Nico. "I'll be all right."

Wolf grinned his cruel, silver grin.

"Get lost," he said. "Or I'll set my Wolf Boys on you."

Tid tugged at Danny's arm. Danny looked down. Tid's face was white and terrified. And Danny knew that he didn't have a choice. He had to get Tid to safety. "Then I'll come back," he told himself. "And that's a promise."

He looked up at Nico. Nico still wouldn't meet his eyes. Wolf drummed his boots on the tombstone. He was waiting for them to go. He wasn't interested in them any more. This was between him and Nico.

Danny took Tid's arm and led him stumbling towards the cemetery gates.

Nico waited until they were out of hearing.

Then he shrugged. "They're not worth it," he told Wolf. "They're not worth the effort. They're not in your league. They're not anywhere near it. Just forget about them."

Wolf knew his Wolf Boys were watching him, to see what he would do.

"Maybe you're right," he said to Nico, his voice deliberately cool. He didn't want to fight Nico for his cap. He wasn't sure if he would win.

And Nico saw it – the uncertainty in Wolf's eyes.

"Have your cap back," he said to Wolf. "Doesn't suit me anyway."

He took off the cap and held it out to Wolf. Wolf glanced at it but he didn't take it.

Outside the railings Danny's mum grabbed Tid and hugged him so tight he could hardly breathe. "How could you let your little brother get mixed up in this?" she hissed at Danny. "You and that wicked Sebastian – what kind of example are you?"

Danny opened his mouth. He closed it again. What was the use? Then he turned round and began walking towards the cemetery gates.

"Where are you going?" his mum demanded.

"I'm keeping a promise."

"What are you talking about!"

"Nico's still in there. I'm going back in."

"No you're not. You're coming home with me."

But Danny didn't turn back.

Inside the graveyard, one small part of Nico's brain was wishing, "Don't come back in, Danny. Don't come back in." But mostly, he was concentrating on Wolf.

Wolf looked at the cap. He looked again at Nico,

sizing him up. He thought about the hammer hidden in Nico's coat. Then he took the cap and fitted it back on his own head. It was too big for him now that Nico had worn it. But he didn't take it off and make it smaller.

"Got something else of yours," said Nico. He took the hammer out of his belt and handed it back to Wolf, handle first.

Wolf nodded. "Want to be a Wolf Boy?" he asked Nico.

Nico knew he had to answer very carefully.

"I don't take orders good," said Nico. "You wouldn't want me."

And, to his relief, Wolf nodded again, as if he understood.

Nico turned around. He could almost feel Wolf's eyes burning into his back. He heard the Wolf Boys shuffling forward, waiting to be let off the leash. But Wolf didn't give any orders. Nico walked free out of the cemetery. And bumped into Danny, on his way back in, keeping his promise.

"He let you go!" said Danny, amazed. He peered back into the cemetery.

"It's all right," said Nico. "They're not coming after me."

"Did you have to fight Wolf?"

"Naa," said Nico. "I had to give him his cap back though."

Danny said nothing. He didn't mind too much about the cap. He could never have worn it again anyway. He couldn't believe he'd defied Wolf and refused to hand it over. Did he really do that?

"Stupid," he thought, shaking his head. "If Nico hadn't turned up you'd be dogmeat now."

But he couldn't help feeling a sneaky glow of pride.

Tid came running up: "Wolf is scary, isn't he, Nico?"

"He's a scumbag," said Nico. Then he said, "But we better get away from here. Case he changes his mind about letting us go."

"Mum's got the car," said Danny.

Nico peered uneasily up the road to where Danny's mum was waiting. "Think I'll walk," he said.

"I'll walk with you then," said Danny.

As they were trudging down Eagle Road Danny's mum pulled up beside them in the car. She rolled the window down.

"Get in," she said.

Nico began walking off on his own. But Danny's mum said, "You too, Nico. I'll give you a lift."

"I'm all right."

"Get in. Please."

In the car no one spoke. Tid was breathing easy for the first time in weeks. But the burn marks on his neck were still sore. He reached up a hand to pat them. He wouldn't forget Wolf for a long, long time. Maybe never.

Nico was thinking about the seagull, wondering if it had survived the day.

Danny was thinking about the same thing. He whispered, "Can I come and see that seagull?"

Danny's mum heard them whispering.

"Danny," she said, "I don't know what's been going on. But you've got to promise me never, ever to see Sebastian again. Can you promise me that?"

"Absolutely," said Danny, raising his eyebrows at Nico. "Far as I'm concerned, Sebastian doesn't exist."

"Good," sighed Mum, as she turned out of Eagle Road.

Danny was sick of Sebastian anyway. Sick of lying about who was his real friend. Every time he did it it seemed like a betrayal of Nico. He didn't want to do that any more. Even if it caused big trouble with his mum.

But then Mum said a surprising thing. She said,

"Nico can have his tea at our house – if he likes."

It was Nico's turn to raise his eyebrows. "You sure, Mrs Jackson?" Nico had never been asked to stay for tea at anyone's house.

"So what do you like to eat?" enquired Danny's mum.

"What, me?" said Nico. "You don't have to worry about me, Mrs Jackson. I'm not fussy. I'll eat anything. Just anything."

"Nico," said Danny's mum, "you can come to tea any time you like."

Epilogue

It was the first day of the summer holidays. Danny, Nico and Tid were at the council rubbish tip. They stood looking in through the wire.

It was like a moonscape in there. Yellow JCBs jerked about in clouds of dust. Lorries trundled in and out. Scraps of paper blew everywhere and plastered themselves to the wire fence.

Danny wrinkled his nose. The tip smelled like a stinking bonfire. "It's not very . . . beautiful, is it?" he said.

"Pardon?" said Nico.

At Nico's feet something scuffled in a cardboard box. It was the seagull. Its wing was fixed and today they were setting it free.

"Will it be able to fly?" Danny had asked Nico that morning.

"Dunno," Nico had said. "Wings are complicated things. Depends if it's mended right."

But Danny had imagined them letting it go somewhere beautiful. He had imagined a glittering sea and foamy waves and the gull soaring into a blue sky. Not a smelly council rubbish tip.

"Gulls like rubbish tips," said Nico. "Look out there."

Nico was right. Snowstorms of squawking gulls followed every JCB and lorry.

"This is where all his friends are," said Tid.

Nico pulled on some old leather gloves. He opened up the cardboard box. The gull was no longer a sad bundle of feathers. As soon as Nico lifted the lid it poked its yellow hatchet beak out of the gap.

"Ouch," said Nico as it tried to peck his wrist.

"You could keep it as a pet," said Tid.

"No way," said Nico. "It's a wild creature. It wants to be set free. Besides, it's got some very nasty habits. You know the fish I feed it? Well, it sicks it up all over the place and my mum doesn't like it."

"Really?" asked Danny, surprised. Somehow, he'd got the idea that Nico's mum was so easy-going, compared to his own, that Nico could do anything he wanted.

Tid put a hand up to his neck. It was just an automatic gesture really. The scars were fading. But he still dreamed about a creature with silver teeth and yellow eyes. Sometimes it was a wolf. Sometimes it was a giant spider that trapped him in a sticky web that he couldn't escape from.

"Make the seagull fly," he said to Nico.

Nico knew that, ever since he'd walked out of the cemetery in one piece, Tid thought he could work miracles. But he had to say, "I can't promise. It might not be able to."

And, if it couldn't, Nico thought privately, it would be kinder to kill it than to keep it shut up in a shed, dragging a crippled wing around for the rest of its life.

Danny was in a good mood today. Mum had stopped playing detective. She had got a new job. She'd said to Danny, "It's a really good chance. I'm not sure whether to take it though. It means less time for you and Tid." And Danny said, "Take it, take it! Don't worry about me and Tid. We can look after ourselves."

She still talked about Sebastian sometimes. Still thought he was the world's worst villain. When she walked past the florist's in the shopping mall she always sighed and shook her head. "That poor woman, with an awful son like that! Compared to Sebastian," she thought, "my Danny seems like a saint."

Danny hadn't seen Wolf since the cemetery. And that was weeks ago now. No one had been following him. Once he thought he saw the flash of a silver star in the shopping mall. But he was probably imagining it. He made sure he didn't walk down Eagle Road though. He didn't want to push his luck.

Nico took the seagull out of its box. It squirmed in his grip and stabbed his gloves.

"All right, all right," said Nico, trying to soothe it.

He held his hands high up in the air.

Tid held his breath. Nico let the seagull go.

Flop, it tumbled down into the mud.

"Oh no," thought Nico, watching Tid's face fall from hope to crushing disappointment.

"You promised!" Tid roared at Nico. "You promised!"

"No, I didn't," said Nico.

Tid transferred his anger to the gull.

"Fly!" he bawled at it. He was almost in tears. "You fly!"

"Shut up, Tid," said Danny. "Give it a chance."

The gull flexed its stiff wings. It hopped and fluttered.

Then, suddenly, it took off.

"It's flying, it's flying!" cried Tid, dancing around and pointing. "Look at that!"

The gull soared above the fence like a giant white butterfly.

Danny didn't dance around. That was too uncool – that was for little brothers. But his face was one huge grin.

"Phew," thought Nico. He was more surprised than they were. He knew that sick wild creatures often die on you. You thought you knew how to save them. But you didn't.

"Gulls are tough," he told Tid, as they watched it flap over the rubbish tip. "They're survivors."

They watched their gull until it joined a swirling flock of birds around a JCB. Then they couldn't pick it out any more.

They stood in silence for a minute.

"So what do we do now?" said Nico.

"I'm starving," said Tid. "Let's go and get something to eat."

"Avocado soup anyone?" asked Danny.

"Is that supposed to be funny?" said Tid.

"Not really." Danny gave an apologetic grin. "Nothing about Sebastian was very funny."

"You know, you're right!" said Nico, as if he'd just made a big discovery. "That's what I couldn't stand about him! He had no sense of humour."

He chucked the empty cardboard box over the wire. He peeled off the leather gloves and stuffed them into his pocket. Then joined the others for the long walk home.